Summer W

Becky Johnson
Illustrated by Ashley Marie Reynolds

Formatted by Katie Erickson.

ISBN-13: 978-1493574216
ISBN-10: 1493574213

Published by Create Space

I dedicate this
book to my inspirations:
Erik & Ashley,
and my treasures:
Zoey, Lily, and Nolan
B.J.

Each wish is for you!
Bucky Johnson

To the
dream chasers.
A.M.R.

Dreum big, Scarlette
AMR

I hope you're excited that summer is here.

What adventures await to discover, my dear?

I hope you wish upon a star,

and see a rainbow from afar.

I hope you find joy in the sprouting of seeds,

as you grow your own garden,
everything but weeds.

I hope you spy a butterfly,

and see the fireworks in July.

I hope that nature is your friend,

with endless wonders around each bend.

I hope you gaze at a firefly,

and ponder, amazed at the
brilliant night sky!

I hope you find shade for a picnic spot,

skip stones in a stream,
then wade in when you're hot!

I hope you camp out under a full moon,

roast marshmallows, eat s'mores,
and not wake until noon!

I hope you build sand castles at the beach,

climb dunes, hunt shells,
the most special within reach!

I hope your summer's filled with
watermelon and ice cream,

and lots of time to sit and dream.

Summer was great with adventure galore.

Fall's on its way. Come on, let's explore!

Check out the other books in this series!

Fall Wishes

Winter Wishes

Spring Wishes

Coming soon!

Meet the author!

Becky spent much of her childhood in the great north woods of Drummond Island, Michigan. As an adult and mother, she shared her beloved island with her two children and husband. Much of this book is based off the simple summertime pleasures that took place at Drummond Island. Becky is a dedicated teacher who always encourages her students to use their imaginations. These are her summer wishes to children everywhere!

Meet the illustrator!

Ashley has loved drawing for as long as she can remember! The puppy in this book is based off her daughter's treasured stuffed animal, who went on all family adventures. Ashley loved bringing 'Babesters' to life and expressing his emotions throughout the summertime escapades!

68977329R00018

Made in the USA
Lexington, KY
23 October 2017